"No!" Salem yelled. "My pizza!"

He sprang onto the table, hissing and spitting.

"Ye-e-o-o-w-l!" The kitten flew out of the box and skittered off the table. She left a trail of little red paw prints behind.

Salem pushed open the lid to the box with his nose. "Oh no," he wailed. He couldn't believe it. She'd eaten every single anchovy. Every slice of pepperoni. Every crumb of sausage.

She stole his people. She stole his mouse. Now she'd stolen his food. Where would it all end?

Story Link®
Program

Sabrina, the Teenage Witch™
Salem's Tails™

Available from MINSTREL Books

Sabrina The Teenage Witch™

Salem's Tails™

CAT BY THE TAIL

Sarah J. Verney

Based on Characters Appearing in Archie Comics

And based upon the television series
Sabrina, The Teenage Witch
Created for television by Nell Scovell
Developed for television by Jonathan Schmock

Illustrated by Mark Dubowski

A MINSTREL® BOOK

Published by POCKET BOOKS
New York   London   Toronto   Sydney   Tokyo   Singapore

This book is a work of fiction. Names, characters, places and incidents are products of the author's imagination or are used fictitiously. Any resemblance to actual events or locales or persons living or dead is entirely coincidental.

A MINSTREL PAPERBACK *Original*

A Minstrel Book published by
POCKET BOOKS, a division of Simon & Schuster Inc.
1230 Avenue of the Americas, New York, NY 10020

Salem Quotes taken from the following episodes:
Pilot—Teleplay by Nell Scovell
      Television Story by Barney Cohen & Kathryn Wallack
"Trial by Fury" written by Nell Scovell & Norma Safford Vela

ISBN: 0-671-02383-7

First Minstrel Books printing July 1999

10 9 8 7 6 5 4 3 2 1

A MINSTREL BOOK and colophon are registered trademarks of Simon & Schuster Inc.

SABRINA THE TEENAGE WITCH and all related titles, logos and characters are trademarks of Archie Comics Publications, Inc.

Cover photo by Pat Hill Studio; kitten by Ron Kimball

Printed in the U.S.A.

For Evan, Lucas, and Abigail

I'd be nervous if I weren't so good-looking.

—Salem

Chapter 1

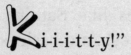i-i-i-t-t-y!"

The loud squeal hurt Salem's ears. He moved as far back into the corner under the bed as possible. Two chubby little hands appeared under the bedspread, followed by a curly blond head.

"Ki-i-i-i-t-t-y!" the wet little mouth squealed again. The hands reached for him.

A small child! Ugh! How could Sabrina, his person and a teenage witch at that, do this to him? He tried to squeeze himself into a small ball. Not that he was *that* big—he was a cat, after all. A black domestic American shorthair, to be exact.

One little hand swiped his fur. It was more than he could stand! "Sabrina!" Salem yelled. "Help!"

He wasn't supposed to talk in front of mortals, just witches like Sabrina. But this was an emergency! And besides, this mortal was too little to know that real cats did not talk.

"Wow!" The child shrieked in surprise and delight. "Da kitty talk!"

Oops. Maybe she wasn't *that* little. *Oh well.* At least no one would believe her if she tried to tell him he could talk. Not in a hundred years.

Salem suddenly smiled to himself. A hundred years! By the time a hundred years passed, he'd be a powerful warlock again! *If only I had my powers now,* he thought. *This little tyke would be a dustbunny.* Of course, if he had his powers back, he wouldn't be cowering under a bed. He'd be taking over the world. . . .

No, no, no. I can't do that. Not right away, anyway. That was how he'd become a cat in the first place. Drell, the head of the Witches' Council, hadn't liked Salem's plan to put himself in charge of the world. So he'd sentenced him to a hundred years as a cat.

And now look at me! Trapped between a wall and a slobbery, babbling child!

"Ki-i-i-t-t-y!" The tiny terror wiggled on her belly, closing the space between them. She grabbed for him again, just missing. Salem hissed at her. The chubby little hand struck again, this time closing around fur. She pulled. Hard.

Ouch! *That's quite enough of that!* Salem thought. *I'm outta here!* He pushed past her. Dashing out from under the bed, he made a beeline for the door.

A wail of protest rose behind him.

Yikes! Salem skidded to a stop. *The door is closed! How did that happen?* He looked around, then launched himself onto Sabrina's dresser.

Salem watched warily as the toddler wriggled out from under the bed. She pushed herself into a standing position and wobbled toward him. "Kitty talk," she said.

"You bet I'll talk more," Salem muttered. "Sa-bri-na!" he yelled. "Open the door!"

The toddler advanced on him, hands out. Salem looked around in a panic. *Where to now?* He needed someplace high. But he couldn't reach the top of the bookcase from here. . . .

The toddler poked him, then grabbed hold of his fur with both hands. "Niiice kiiitty," she said. She tried to lift him.

"Yeeow!" *That's it!* Salem thought. *No more Mr. Nice Cat!* He hissed and raised one paw up high, claws out, ready to strike.

"SALEM! Don't you dare. She's just a baby." Salem looked up and saw Sabrina in the open doorway. She held the hand of another small child.

" 'Brina!" the toddler said happily. She let go of Salem's fur and toddled over to Sabrina.

"Baby! Hhmmph!" Salem snorted. He licked his ruffled fur. "Miniature terrorist, you mean." He looked at the small boy holding Sabrina's hand. He shuddered. "There are *two* of them?"

"Uh-huh," Sabrina said. "The Beaumont twins. From down the street."

"Tell me they aren't staying," Salem begged.

"Okay. They aren't staying," Sabrina said. "Their mother will be back any minute now. I'm just baby-sitting."

"Well, sit on them harder, would you please?" Salem nodded at the little girl. "That one escaped. I was peacefully contemplating important world affairs. . . ."

"You mean you were sleeping," Sabrina corrected.

"Whatever. And then that . . . that . . . *thing* appeared out of nowhere and cornered me. Somehow, the door got shut. I was trapped."

"Sorry," Sabrina said. "Ryan went after Aunt Zelda's labtop. I had to get him away from it. And the minute my back was turned, Abigail wandered off." She sighed. "Babies are a lot of work."

"Kitty talkin'," the little boy said.

Sabrina looked nervous. "Maybe we shouldn't be having this conversation right now," she said.

"No problem. I'll gladly go someplace else," Salem said. He held his tail high and walked past Sabrina. "Someplace peaceful. Someplace where there are no babies."

"Kitty says me-ow, right, Ryan?" Sabrina said as Salem walked out the door.

"Uh-uh," Salem said under his breath. "Right now, Kitty says bye-bye." *Babies! Ugh!* he thought. *Thank goodness we don't have any of those living here!*

Chapter 2

Oh, we love Salem, yes we do,
He's our leader, through and through
Salem, Salem, you're so fine
You truly are a leader di-viiiine!

Salem tapped a paw in time to the music. It was such a beautiful song. He bestowed a royal nod on his devoted followers. They cheered and applauded wildly. *Ah, life is sweet,* Salem thought. But suddenly the voices turned squeaky and shrill. His ears began to hurt. And then, before his very eyes, his loyal followers all turned to whining, crying babies. . . .

Salem's eyes popped open. He shuddered. *It was just a dream,* he told himself. *A nightmare.* He was safe in his own living room, far from those horrible babies.

Salem stretched. He yawned.

E-e-e-e-e-k!

Wait a minute! What was that?

E-e-e-e-k!

What was that squeak? Salem stopped stretching and looked slowly around the room. He saw Zelda on the couch, reading a huge science text. His eye roamed over chairs, piano, table . . . all normal.

Then he saw it. Salem froze. He couldn't believe his eyes. It couldn't be! Not in his house! It was just too awful!

"Who let that . . . that . . . that . . . *kitten* in here?" he demanded.

"E-e-e-e-o-w." As if it had just been waiting to be noticed, the little peach-colored ball of fuzz trotted over to Salem. It gazed adoringly up at him. A rumble began deep inside the kitten, making its entire little body vibrate. She was purring.

Salem took two giant steps back. "Hey!" he said loudly. "I said, who let that hairball in here?"

Sabrina bounced down the stairs, a jacket slung over her arm. "Hairball?" she said. "It must be yours, Salem. I think you're the only one in this house who . . . uh . . . *comes up* with such things." She giggled.

"Not that kind of hairball! This, this . . ." Salem sputtered. "This one. This, this *kitten* . . ."

"Salem, *please!* Can't you keep the noise down? I'm trying to work here." Zelda looked up from her book, peering at him through her glasses.

Sabrina walked over to the kitten and knelt on the floor next to it. "You don't mean this little cutie-pie, do you?" she asked. "Salem, I'm surprised at you. Insulting such a sweet little thing."

"E-e-e-e-k." The kitten took several steps toward Salem. She rubbed her tiny head against his front legs.

"Aww, look," Sabrina said. "Isn't that cute, Salem? She likes you! She's marking you with her scent. That's what it means when cats do . . ."

"I know that!" Salem snapped. "I'm a cat, remember?" He backed away from the kitten.

Zelda put her book down and joined them. "She *is* awfully sweet," she said.

She picked the kitten up. "I don't think I've ever heard a kitten purr quite this loud."

"Hey, I want to hold her," Sabrina said. She took the kitten from Zelda and cradled her in one hand. "Oooh, look how tiny she is," she exclaimed.

"You could put a spell on her and make her even tinier," Salem suggested. "Then someone might step on her. Squash her like a bug."

Sabrina and her aunt ignored him.

"She is adorable, isn't she?" Aunt Hilda said, joining them from the kitchen. She took the kitten from Sabrina. "Isn't she a widdle tweetie-pie?" she asked. She rubbed noses with the kitten. "A widdle snookie-wookums . . ."

"Oh, please, spare me," Salem muttered. "I think I'm going to hock up a major hairball here." He gagged loudly.

The Spellman women paid him no attention. Sabrina and Zelda crowded around Hilda. They stroked the kitten, making kissing noises and talking baby talk.

"Excuse me!" Salem said loudly. "Could someone *please* tell me where that thing came from?"

"Let *me* hold her now," Zelda said.

"But I want to hold her again," Sabrina said. "I only got her for a minute."

"*Ahem!*" Salem tried again. "What's the hairball doing here, anyway?"

They ignored him.

"*Okay,*" Salem said at last, as loud as he could. "Don't tell me how it got here. Actually, I don't really care. Just take it back where it belongs. Like NOW!"

Hilda looked up from the little ball of fluff in her hands. "Why Salem," she said, surprised. "I do believe you're jealous."

13

"Don't be ridiculous," Salem snapped. He casually licked a paw to show how unconcerned he was.

"Well, you needn't worry, you know," Hilda said. "I found her outside when I took out the trash. It was raining, and she was soaked. I only brought her in to get her dry. It's not like she's moving in."

"She must belong to one of the neighbors," Zelda put in. "We'll ask around as soon as the storm lets up."

"Don't worry, Salem," Sabrina said. "This kitten must belong to someone. She's so cute. I'll bet someone is looking for her right now." She patted Salem on the head. "But I think it's sweet that you're jealous."

"I am *not* jealous," Salem protested. "I just don't think we need a baby in the house. They're a lot of trouble, you know. They get into things they're not supposed to. They break things. You should know that," he said to Sabrina. "Remember the twins?"

"But Salem, this is a baby *cat*, not a baby *baby*," Sabrina said. "It's different. Kittens are easy to take care of. No trouble at all."

"Humph!" Salem snorted. "That shows how much *you* know. Mark my words. Get that kitten out of here, or there will be trouble. Big trouble."

15

Chapter 3

"There, that should do it." Sabrina used her magic to stick another "found" poster to a telephone pole. "That's ten posters. We'll find the kitten's owner in no time."

"I sure hope so," Salem grumbled from inside her backpack. He'd come along to make sure the posters got put up properly. No way he was going to leave this thing to chance.

"I thought you weren't jealous," Sabrina teased him.

"I'm not," Salem said. "It's just that . . . uh . . . I just don't want her to get homesick, that's all," he finished. "Poor little hairb . . . I mean, baby."

Sabrina looked around to make sure no one was watching, then zapped them both back home again.

The kitten ran up to them, her tiny tail straight in the air. She was mewing wildly.

"Hi there, cute stuff," Sabrina said. She picked the kitten up and stroked her head. "Did ums get wonesome when Sabrina and Salem went bye-bye?" She slid her backpack off her shoulder. It landed on the floor with a *thud*.

"Ouch!" Salem protested. "Watch it!"

"Oops! Sorry, Salem," Sabrina said. "I guess I kinda forgot you were in there."

"Gee, thanks," Salem grumbled. He jumped out of the pack. *All that kitten has to do is show up, and I'm forgotten.*

Salem jumped up onto the table and swatted at the phone. The receiver fell off. "I'd better call the newspaper, too," Salem said, "and put an ad in the Lost and Found."

"Done," Hilda said, coming down the stairs. She hung the phone back up. "It's all taken care of, Salem. There's nothing left to do but wait for the phone to ring."

"Oh." Salem flicked his tail back and forth. "Isn't there something else we can do?" he asked.

"Nothing I can think of," said Hilda.

"Me neither," Sabrina added.

"You're sure you don't want to cast a finding spell to locate her owner?" Salem asked. "Just a little one?"

"Oh no, no way," Sabrina said. She shook her head. "You remember the trouble I got into the first time I used a locater spell. I almost ended up married to a troll. Forget it. We'll find her owner the mortal way." She set the kitten on the floor.

"Darn." Salem sighed. He jumped off the table and wandered toward the couch. "I guess there's nothing else to do, then." He yawned. "It must be time for a nap, in that case."

"You always think it's time for a nap," Sabrina said.

Salem jumped onto the couch and curled up, getting comfortable. He closed his eyes. Seconds later, he opened them again. Something wasn't right.

The kitten was inches from his face. She had settled herself right next to him. Purring loudly, she began to knead her tiny paws into his chest.

Salem pushed the kitten away with one paw. "I'm not your mama. Get out of my face, fuzz-brain."

The kitten purred louder. Salem pushed her harder. "Get up," he insisted. "This is *my* spot."

The kitten closed her eyes and purred louder. She didn't budge.

"Aw, Salem, leave her alone." Hilda said. "She's so cute. And she likes you."

"Yippee," Salem replied sourly. He pushed the kitten with his nose. "Come on, hairball, I said outta here." The kitten raised her head and gazed at him. Her eyes shone with adoration.

"You know, Salem, she really does think you're the greatest," Hilda commented. "Look at the way she's looking at you. That's pure love in those baby blues."

"So she recognizes a superior being when she sees one," Salem said. "She ought to show some respect. Go, you little pest." He pushed the kitten hard. She tumbled off the couch.

Hilda swooped in and scooped the kitten up. "Salem, that was downright mean," she scolded. She nuzzled the kitten with her nose. "Come on, sweetie-kins," she cooed. "Don't pay any attention to that big, bad Salem." She scratched the kitten under the chin.

Salem sighed. Nobody had scratched under his chin all day. Or stroked his back. *Not since that little pest arrived.* He closed his eyes, grumbling to himself.

"Ooh, you like that, don't you, honey-bun?" Hilda said. "Listen to that little motor go."

Salem opened one eye. He watched

21

Hilda carry the kitten away, still cooing at her.

Crazy witch, he thought. *Making such a fuss over a hairball.*

Well, let her. He didn't care.

Much.

Chapter 4

Salem knocked the phone receiver off its cradle with his paw. Then he slowly punched in the number of a local pizza place. One that delivered, of course.

"Hello, Pizza Napoli? Yes, I'd like to order a medium pizza, please. Pepperoni, sausage, and double anchovies. To be delivered to the Spellman residence. And make it snappy!"

Salem smiled to himself as he pushed

the receiver back on its cradle. He could imagine what the woman on the other end would say if she knew she was talking to a cat!

Salem trotted up the stairs. *I wonder what Sabrina is up to,* he thought.

He found her standing in front of her mirror. She zapped herself into an outfit, studied it, and frowned. Then she did it again. And again.

The kitten was in Sabrina's room too. She was racing around the bed, playing with a small catnip mouse.

"Hey, that's my mouse," Salem protested.

"Oh, Salem, let her play with it," Sabrina said, sounding irritated. "What do you care?" She zapped herself into another outfit.

Salem opened his mouth to tell her that he *did* care. Instead, though, he

24

snapped it shut again. *What's the use?* Sabrina would never take his side. She liked that stupid hairball too much.

Sabrina zapped herself into yet another outfit.

"Let me guess," Salem said. "You're going out with Harvey tonight?"

Sabrina nodded. "Yeah. There's a dance at the school."

"So why the fashion show? Doesn't lover boy always think you're gorgeous?"

Sabrina plopped down on the bed. "I wish. Lately, he just can't seem to keep his eyes off this new exchange student." She sighed. "I don't like the way he looks at her, Salem. He's only supposed to look at *me* like that. Of course she'll be there tonight. Looking like a model."

She stood and faced the mirror again. "I've got to come up with something so gorgeous he won't even see her." She zapped herself into another outfit.

"Sabrina, Sabrina, Sabrina," Salem said slowly. "You're a witch, remember? You don't need a new outfit. You just need to outfox the fox."

"But how?" Sabrina asked.

"Well . . . how about some See Me dust?" Salem suggested.

"See Me dust?"

"Yeah. Just blow some in Harvey's direction, and he won't be able to take his eyes off you. All night."

"It sounds good, but . . ."

"But what?"

"I haven't got much time," Sabrina said. "Can I make it fast?"

"No problem," Salem said. "The recipe is in the book."

Sabrina pulled out *The Discovery of Magic*, a huge book of spells. She sat cross-legged on the bed, the book in front of her. The kitten forgot about the catnip mouse and crawled into Sabrina's lap, purring. Sabrina absent-mindedly stroked the baby's head as she flipped through the pages.

Salem jumped up on the bed next to Sabrina, reading along with her. He wished she was scratching *his* head.

A few minutes later the doorbell rang. Sabrina jumped. "Oh no! That's probably Harvey!" she cried. "I'm not ready yet!"

"Relax," Salem said. "I bet that's just my pizza. Uh . . . could you get it for me?" he asked. "The money is on the table downstairs."

"But I've got to find that spell! Harvey will be here any minute."

"I'll look for it," Salem promised. He turned over another page with his paw.

Sabrina left the room, taking the kitten with her.

"See Me dust, See Me dust . . ." Salem muttered. "It's got to be here somewhere . . ."

"Did you find it yet?" Sabrina asked, appearing in the doorway a minute later.

"Yep. Here it is. See Me dust. You need some octopus eyeballs and some toad toenails and . . ."

"Eww, gross. Oh well, I guess you gotta do what you gotta do," Sabrina said. She took the book from Salem. He waited for her to thank him. Or to tell him how wonderful he was. But she didn't. She just got to work on her spell.

Salem's stomach growled loudly. "I guess I'll go eat that pizza," he said. "Unless you, uh, might need me for anything . . ."

"Oh, no, that's okay," Sabrina said. She didn't even look up from the book.

Salem trotted out into the hall and headed down the steps, his tail drooping. As the smell of pepperoni reached him, though, he began to feel more cheerful. Maybe that kitten had stolen his catnip mouse. Maybe Sabrina didn't appreciate him. *But there's a whole pizza waiting for me. How bad could things be?*

Salem picked up speed as he went through the dining room. Almost there! He raced through the door to the kitchen.

Suddenly Salem stopped dead in his tracks. He could see the pizza box on the kitchen table. The lid was half open, bobbing up and down. A tiny peach-colored tail peeked out.

"No!" Salem yelled. "My pizza!" He sprang onto the table, hissing and spitting.

"Ye-e-o-o-w-l!" The kitten flew out of

29

the box and skittered off the table. She left a trail of little red paw prints behind.

Salem pushed open the lid to the box with his nose. "Oh no," he wailed. He couldn't believe it. She'd eaten every single anchovy. Every slice of pepperoni. Every crumb of sausage.

She stole his people. She stole his mouse. Now she'd stolen his food. Where would it all end?

Chapter 5

Something tapped the tip of Salem's tail. *Oh no! Not her again!* He flicked his tail away, annoyed.

He'd ignore her. She'd go away. He wouldn't even look at her.

Whap! She batted his tail again. He flicked it away again.

Whap, whap, whap!

Flick, flick, flick.

Whap, whap, whap.

Salem growled, deep in his throat.

31

The kitten growled back at him.

Salem opened one eye and growled again, louder. The kitten backed up three steps, wiggled her rear, and pounced. She landed smack on his tail, opened her little mouth and—*Yeow!* Salem jumped a foot in the air. *She bit me!*

That does it. I'm not taking this! I'll show her!

The kitten bolted off the couch. Salem took off after her, up the stairs, past the linen closet, around Sabrina's room, back out in the hall . . . Salem stopped, panting hard. *Whew! I'm not used to this!*

No time to rest now. She was getting away from him!

The kitten shot back down the stairs. Salem dashed after her.

Oh no! Where'd she go?

Salem ran toward the kitchen. She must be in there.

"Well, hello there!"

Sabrina! Salem skidded to a stop at the sound of her voice. She hadn't seen him dashing through the house like that, had she? *How undignified. How embarrassing!*

He took a deep breath. He licked a paw and smoothed down some ruffled fur. Then he strolled casually into the kitchen.

"Hey there, precious. How ya doin'?" Sabrina said. She sat at the kitchen table, eating a bowl of ice cream. *Precious?* She'd never called him *that* before. *But hey,* Salem thought, *I can live with it. It's about time they showed me some appreciation. And I* am *rather precious. As in valuable. Beloved.*

"Hello, Sabrina," Salem said. He held his head and his tail high.

She turned toward him. "Oh, hi,

Salem," Sabrina said. "I didn't hear you come in."

Salem's tail drooped. The hairball was in Sabrina's lap. She hadn't called *him* precious at all! She'd been talking to that miserable little beast.

"How are things in the cat world?" Sabrina asked.

"Why don't you ask fuzz-face?" Salem grumbled. He should have known. No one around here cared about him anymore. The hairball had taken over.

"Oooh, sounds like somebody got up on the wrong side of the bed today," Sabrina said. "Feeling a little grumpy, are we?"

"Me? Grumpy? Of course not." Salem forced himself to sound cheerful.

As Salem watched miserably, Sabrina gently stroked the kitten's back. Then she dipped her finger in her ice cream and offered it to the kitten. The kitten lapped it up. *No surprise there,* Salem thought.

"You like that, babycakes?" Sabrina asked. "Here you go, then," Sabrina said. She set her ice cream bowl and the kitten on the floor. The kitten proceeded to lick it clean. Sabrina stroked her back as she ate.

Salem tried to push away the hot feeling that rose up inside him. So what if *his* person was lavishing affection on another cat? So what if he loved ice cream too? *Who cares?* he asked himself silently. "Well, actually, I do," he muttered quietly.

"What? Did you say something, Salem?" Sabrina looked up from the kitten.

Salem cleared his throat noisily. "No. Just a tickle in my throat, that's all."

"Oh. Hey, did anyone call about the kitten while I was at school?" Sabrina asked.

"No," Salem said glumly. "Nobody."

"Hmm. Isn't that strange," Sabrina said. "It's been over a week already. I just don't understand it."

"Don't understand what?" Zelda asked, coming into the kitchen.

"Why no one has called about the kitten," Sabrina said. "I was sure we'd find her owner by now."

"It does seem odd," Zelda said. "Maybe she isn't really lost after all. Maybe she was abandoned."

"But that's so cruel," Sabrina said.

"I know. But it doesn't stop people from doing it," Zelda said looking at her niece over the rim of her glasses.

"What if no one claims her?" Sabrina asked. "We can't just throw her back outside to fend for herself." She picked the kitten up and hugged her to her chest.

"Of course not," Zelda assured her. "If no one comes looking for her, we'll find her a good home," she said firmly. "We can't keep her."

"I don't see why not," Sabrina said. "She's no trouble."

"That's not really the point, Sabrina. Witches don't have mortal pets. We have familiars."

Sabrina knew a familiar was an animated object. In the Spellman household that was Salem, the talking cat.

"That's true," Salem said. He didn't like where this conversation was leading. "It wouldn't be right."

"Why not?" Sabrina asked. "Does the Witches' Council have some rule against it?"

"Well, no," Zelda said. "It's simply not done, that's all." She pointed at the ice cream dish. It rose in the air and floated to the kitchen sink. "You shouldn't be feeding her ice cream, you know," she added. "It's not good for her."

Sabrina scratched the kitten behind her ears. "Okay, I won't feed her ice cream anymore. And I'll be responsible for her, I promise. You won't have to do anything. I'll feed her and clean her litter box." Sabrina quickly pointed up a bowl of kitten food. "See? It's easy."

"It's not just a question of who will take care of her," Zelda said. "What about Salem? Bringing another cat into the house wouldn't be fair to him."

"It wouldn't?" Salem asked. "I mean, you're right. Of course it wouldn't."

"Cats are very territorial," Zelda added. "They don't like sharing their space. They get very jealous. Especially when they're older."

"Hey, who are you calling old?" Salem protested. "I'm not old. And I'm not jealous, either. I—"

"See," Sabrina interrupted, "he doesn't care. Salem isn't an ordinary cat."

"That's right," Salem said. "I'm a warlock. A relatively *young*—"

"Oh, please, Aunt Zelda," Sabrina interrupted. "Let me keep her. I'll take care of her, I promise. We can't just give her away to someone we don't even know."

"As a matter of fact," Salem went on, "I'd say I'm in my prime. As a cat or a warlock. I've never been in better shape and—"

"Of course not, Salem," Zelda said. She patted him absently on the head. "I don't know," she said to Sabrina. "We'll see. Maybe."

Salem's mouth dropped open in surprise. *What?* Had he heard right? Had Zelda practically agreed to keep the kitten?

Oh no! I have to stop this!
But how?

Chapter 6

The kitten dashed frantically around in a circle. Once, twice, three times around. She stopped and batted at her tail. She caught it and rolled onto her back. Holding her tail between her paws, she snapped at it. Seconds later, she jumped up and began chasing her tail again, as if she'd never seen it before.

Salem chuckled. "You really do have fuzz for brains," he said. "Don't you know that thing is attached to you?"

4 1

The kitten stopped and looked at him. Then she took off across the room, zig-zagging wildly. Finally she pounced on a small crumpled piece of paper. She batted it, chased it, batted it again, then threw it up in the air. When it landed, she pounced on it.

"Whew," Salem said. He put his head down. "I get worn out just *watching* you."

The kitten picked up the piece of paper in her mouth and trotted over to Salem, tail high.

She jumped onto the couch and dropped the paper inches from his nose. "Gee, thanks," Salem said. "I've always wanted a dead piece of paper."

The kitten pushed her head against his face, purring loudly.

"Hey, cool it, fish-breath," Salem said. "Not so close."

Suddenly there was a shriek from upstairs. Salem jumped.

Sabrina appeared at the top of the stairs. *"Sa-lem!* You get up here right now!" she yelled.

"Uh-oh," Salem said. "I don't like the sound of that." He looked around. "How come there's never anyone around to open the door when I need to make a quick exit?"

"Sa-lem!" Sabrina yelled again. She thundered down the stairs. "Why did you do this?" she asked. She waved a fistful of shredded papers at him.

Salem sat up. Next to him, the kitten perfectly imitated his pose.

"Sabrina, I'm hurt," Salem said. He put on his most mournful face. "I have no idea what you're talking about."

"I'm talking about my history paper," Sabrina said. "The one on Abraham Lincoln. It was sitting on my bed, finished. And now it looks like something that belongs in the bottom of a hamster cage. It's due today, and I have to leave for school in five minutes!" She glared at him.

"That's terrible," Salem said. "But it's not *my* fault."

"Oh no? You're the only one with sharp teeth and claws around here," Sabrina countered.

Salem looked pointedly at the kitten. "Not the only one," he said.

"Oh, come on," Sabrina protested. "Those itty-bitty teeth? Those teeny claws? No way."

"Well, all I can say is that I prefer smoked salmon to processed wood pulp," Salem said, putting his nose in the air. That was true. Salmon did taste much better. But tearing up the paper had been kind of fun.

Sabrina looked doubtful. "Did you do this?" she asked the kitten, shaking the papers at her.

"Mew," the kitten squeaked.

"Sounds like a confession to me," Salem said.

Sabrina picked up the kitten. "Bad kitty!" she said sternly, waving the papers in front of her face. "Bad, bad girl!"

"Sabrina, get a grip," Salem said. "She's just a baby. She can't be held responsible for her actions." He shook his head sadly. "You have to expect this sort of thing. Just be glad it was only your history paper."

"*Only?* It's one-quarter of my grade for the semester! And it's *ruined!*"

"Too bad. Any other day you could just zap it back together," Salem said.

"I know! But I can't!" Sabrina wailed. "I promised Aunt Zelda I wouldn't use magic for anything else on this paper."

"Oh?" Salem said, as if he'd had no idea.

Sabrina sighed. "She wasn't real happy when she found out I did my research by talking to Lincoln himself. She said it gave me an unfair advantage over the rest of the students. So I promised, no more magic on this paper."

"Pity," Salem said.

"Of course," Sabrina said slyly. "Aunt Zelda never has to know . . ." She raised her hand and began to point at the paper.

"I wouldn't if I were you," Salem said quickly. "She has a way of finding these things out, you know."

Sabrina lowered her hand. "She does, doesn't she? But you and I are the only ones who know. And you wouldn't tell, would you?"

"Of course not!" Salem said.

Sabrina raised her hand again.

"Not on purpose, anyway," Salem added quickly. "But have you ever noticed how much I talk in my sleep? Of course, I have no control over what I say . . ."

Sabrina lowered her hand again. She sighed heavily. "I guess I'd better not take a chance."

"And Zelda and Hilda are already gone for the day, so they can't help. Darn," Salem said. "Although I suppose it could have been worse," he added slyly. "What if she'd eaten some of *The Discovery of Magic?* You could have lost some important spells."

Sabrina shuddered. "Please! Don't even *say* that," she said.

"Better be careful, then," Salem said. "Who knows what she'll go after next? You know," he added, trying to sound casual, "it's probably just not a good idea to have a little one in the house. They can be so destructive."

"*You* could have stopped her." Sabrina frowned at Salem. "Where were you when she was chowing down on my history paper?"

Salem tried to shrug, although it wasn't easy with his narrow cat shoulders. "Busy," he said. "Really, Sabrina, you can't expect me to be her babysitter."

"I don't see why not," Sabrina grumbled.

Salem ignored her. "So what are you going to do? Rewrite your whole paper?" Salem said. *That ought to make her plenty mad*, he thought. *Mad enough to kick that kitten out!*

"Oh no," Sabrina said, sighing. "It's not *that* bad, I guess. I've got it on a computer disk. I can print it out at school. But it means I'll have to skip lunch with Harvey."

Darn, Salem thought. *That's not so bad. That little stunt was supposed to ruin your entire day.* He frowned. "You think life as a teenage witch is tough," he said glumly, "you should try it as a cat."

"Yeah, sure. I can see how tough *that* is." She pointed at the kitten. Her eyes were closed, and she was purring loudly. "She's sound asleep sitting up," Sabrina said. "Isn't that adorable?" She picked the kitten up and began to walk away with her. "Aw, babycakes, I can't stay mad at you. You're just too cute."

A sharp pang hit Salem in the gut. At this rate Sabrina would never get mad enough to kick that kitten out.

Salem put his head down. *So much for that idea,* he thought. He frowned.

Suddenly he brightened. Of course, there *was* more than one witch in this house. And Sabrina wasn't even the one who made the decisions.

He'd just have to take his trouble-making to the top.

Chapter 7

$\mathcal{S}$alem eyed the kitchen table. *Someone left the butter dish out this morning,* he thought. *Lucky me.* It was just what he needed. He looked down at the kitten. As usual, she was right by his side.

"Come on, fuzz-brain. Uncle Salem's gonna show you how to get in trouble. Big trouble." He smiled to himself.

The kitten gazed back at him, her eyes full of love and trust.

51

"Yeah, yeah, I know you love me," he said. "So what? You're still a pain in the neck. Come on."

Salem jumped up onto the kitchen table and waited for the kitten to follow. "Come on, fur-face," Salem commanded.

The kitten mewed at him. She paced anxiously back and forth on the floor. "Well, what are you waiting for? Come on. You managed to get up here for that pizza," he reminded her. "You can do it for me."

The kitten mewed again. Salem waited. Finally, she flung herself onto a chair. From there, she managed to snag the tablecloth and scramble up.

"Atta girl," Salem said. "That's the idea." He felt oddly pleased that she'd made it. Almost as if he were proud of her. *Don't be ridiculous*, he told himself. *I'm just glad she's making this so easy.*

Salem knocked the cover off the butter dish with one swipe of his paw. *Yum,* he thought. *Chow time.*

He looked at the kitten next to him. She gazed at him trustingly. "Aw, knock it off, would ya?" Salem said. "You're starting to make me feel guilty." He looked at the butter and hesitated. It wasn't too late to jump off the table and forget the whole thing.

Salem thought about the kitten eating his pizza. And the way Sabrina lavished attention on her. *She has to go,* he reminded himself. He lowered his head and began to eat the butter.

When it was nearly gone, Salem stepped aside. "Go ahead," he told the kitten. "Have some." The kitten sniffed at it, then began to eat. Salem moved around behind her. He hesitated a second, then gave her a good hard push.

Smoosh! The kitten went face-first into the butter. As she pushed herself back up again, she planted two perfect, tiny paw prints in what was left of the butter.

"Way to go, hairball!" Salem said. She looked so confused he had to laugh.

Small gobs of butter clung to the kitten's whiskers. She tilted her head one way, then the other, trying to look at them. Salem cracked up even more.

The kitten tried to bat at the butter on her whiskers. When she couldn't get it, she shook her head so hard she lost her balance. Little bits of butter went flying. Salem couldn't stop laughing. She looked so funny!

The clock in the hall struck two. *Uh-oh*, Salem thought, suddenly serious. *Hilda will be home soon.* He'd better keep his mind on what he was doing, or he'd be caught red-handed.

"Okay, fuzz-brain, outta here," Salem said. He jumped off the table and waited for the kitten to follow. She did, jumping first onto a chair and then to the floor.

"Now for the crowning touch," Salem said. He jumped back up onto the table. He pushed the glass lid to the butter dish to the edge of the table. "Watch out below," he yelled. "Bombs away!" With a flick of his paw, Salem sent the lid sailing to the ground.

Crash! The glass lid shattered into a hundred pieces. Frightened, the kitten shot out of the kitchen. "Atta girl," Salem said. "Leave those little buttery paw prints all over." He looked around in satisfaction, then jumped to the floor.

Carefully avoiding the broken glass, Salem pranced out of the kitchen. There was no sign of the kitten. He brushed away a little pang of guilt.

Good riddance, he told himself. *Right?*

"Tsk, tsk, tsk," Salem said. "What a mess!" He sat on the kitchen counter, looking at the broken butter dish as if he'd never seen it before.

"I'll say." Hilda looked at the tiny paw prints in the butter. "Looks like our little visitor got a bit hungry while we were out."

Salem shook his head in dismay. "Kids these days, they just don't have any manners, you know?"

Hilda looked at him sharply. "And you had nothing to do with it, did you?"

"Moi?" Salem pretended to be insulted. "Certainly not. I prefer my butter with lobster. Besides, look at those tiny paw prints," he added. "I think the culprit is pretty obvious."

"I suppose you're right." Hilda sighed. "I guess I'd better get to work." She pointed at the cover to the butter dish. The glass pieces rose in the air, hung for a moment, then put themselves back together. Then she pointed at the table. A sponge appeared and mopped up the mess.

"Don't forget the footprints in the living room," Salem said.

Hilda sighed again. She headed toward the living room. "Why do I have to do all the cleaning up?" she complained. "I know Sabrina wants to keep this kitten. But what happens when she's not around? *I* get stuck with pointing out the dirty work, of course."

Salem followed her into the living room. "That's a teenager for you," he said. "She wants the fun, but not the responsibility. If I were you, I'd think long and hard about letting her keep that kitten."

"I couldn't agree with you more," Hilda said. She pointed at the greasy spots in the rug, and they disappeared. "But I'm not sure Zelda feels the same way. I think she's seriously considering letting that kitten stay."

Oh, really? Salem thought. *We'll just see about that!*

Chapter 8

Salem lay with his head down, eyes closed, listening. The kitten was curled up next to him, purring softly. For once, Salem hadn't even tried to chase her away. *Only because I need to know where she is*, he told himself. *Not because I like having her next to me.*

Salem could hear Zelda working. She was mixing potions at her labtop. The compact laboratory was her pride and joy.

Leave it for just a minute, Salem commanded her in his mind. *C'mon, Zelda. Just give me a minute alone with the open labtop.*

Finally Zelda did get up and leave the room.

Thank goodness even witches take breaks, Salem thought.

As soon as Zelda was out of the room, Salem jumped up. He grabbed the kitten by the scruff of her neck with his teeth. She mewed once, then hung there, not resisting. Moving as quickly as he could, he carried her over to the labtop. Then he let her go.

Quick as lightning, Salem jumped up and knocked over some test tubes and vials. There was a small explosion, and a puff of green smoke rose in the air.

Salem winced, but didn't stop. He dashed back to the couch. Within seconds, he was curled up and pretending to be asleep. Opening one eye, he checked on the little kitten. She was just starting to walk back in his direction. *Perfect.*

"Oh, no!" Zelda came back into the living room. "You naughty little kitten." She shook a finger at the kitten. "Salem, why didn't you stop her?"

"What?" Salem lifted his head and blinked sleepily. "Stop who? What happened?"

"You know perfectly well what happened," Zelda said. "Cats don't sleep that soundly."

"I'm not your average cat," Salem said. He jumped off the couch and walked over to the labtop. "Quite a mess," he said innocently.

"It sure is. And three hours of work gone down the drain. I'll have to start all over again."

"Tsk, tsk," Salem said. "A pity, isn't it? And all because of one little baby." He tried not to notice the way the kitten rubbed her head against his legs, purring.

Zelda frowned at the kitten. "Too much more of this, and Sabrina can forget about keeping you."

Salem backed away from the kitten. *Hear that, hairball?* He said to himself. *Your days are numbered.*

So why *don't I feel happy?*

Chapter 9

*B*oom! Boom! Boom!

Salem jumped three feet off Sabrina's bed, startled out of a sound sleep. Next to him, the kitten uttered a surprised "mew." He could hear her little heart start to pound. *What is that?* Salem wondered.

Boom! Boom! Boom!

Someone was banging on the front door, he realized. "Whatever happened to ringing the doorbell?" Salem muttered. "You could give a guy a heart attack!"

Salem wandered out to the landing at the top of the stairs. The kitten was close at his heels.

Boom! Boom! Boom! Salem could see the door shaking, the person on the other side was pounding so hard.

The kitten looked up at him and me-owed plaintively. "Aw, don't worry," Salem said. "He can't get in."

Boom! Boom! Boom!

"I *hope.*" Salem paced nervously. "I wish Sabrina or someone else was home."

Boom! Boom!
Crash!

The front door banged open. Salem and the kitten skittered behind a small chest at the top of the stairs. Heart pounding, he peered around it. Who was there?

A man barreled into the house, a huge Doberman at his side. "Hello?" he bellowed. "Anybody home?"

Fear shot through Salem. The man was huge, and he looked mean. The torn-off sleeves of his black T-shirt revealed rippling biceps covered with tattoos. Under the hall light, Salem could see his shaved head gleaming. He held the dog's leash in a black-gloved hand.

"Something tells me these two aren't selling magazines," Salem muttered to the kitten. She stepped out in full view and took two steps toward the stairs. Salem reached out with his paw and pushed her back out of sight. "Don't be a fool," he whispered.

"Anyone home?" the man snarled again.

There was a piece of a paper in the man's hand, Salem noticed. Straining, he

65

could make out a picture of something small and fluffy . . . a kitten! It was one of the posters he and Sabrina had put up!

The Doberman put his nose in the air and sniffed. He barked twice. The sound sent Salem's heart racing. The fur on his back stood up straight.

"I thought so," the man said. "That little tidbit is here somewhere, ain't she, Killer?" the man said. "We'll find her for ya, don't worry."

Tidbit? Salem thought. *As in snack? This dog wants to chow down on fuzz-face?* Salem pushed the kitten farther behind him.

What am I doing? he thought suddenly. *Why am I standing between that huge, slobbering dog and the hairball?* He looked down at the kitten, who gazed up at him adoringly. *This is my big chance to get rid of you,* he thought. *One good push and you're dog chow.*

Salem put one paw on the kitten's back. *Do it!* he told himself. *You'll have your people back. No more crazy witches fawning over a dumb hairball.* He nudged the kitten half-heartedly. She looked up at him and purred.

No more stolen food. No more interrupted naps, he told himself. *C'mon, push!*

The dog barked. Salem jumped, jerking his paw away from the kitten. *I can't do it!* he realized. *I can't feed her to that beast.*

Salem peered nervously down at the dog. Suddenly, the Doberman began barking like crazy. He strained at his leash. He tried to lunge toward the stairs.

"She's up there, isn't she, Killer?" the man asked. He began to fiddle with the clasp on the leash. "Go get her, then. Find her, Killer."

Salem snapped his head back behind the chest. His heart flip-flopped wildly in his chest. *Oh no!* Salem thought. *We're dead meat now. Both of us.* He fought the urge to panic.

As the dog leaped at the stairs, Salem sprang into action. He grabbed the kitten in his teeth and flung her up onto his back. He barely even winced as she dug her claws into his fur. There was no time to worry about the pain now. "Hang on, hairball," Salem said. "You're going for a ride."

As the dog charged up the stairs, Salem and the kitten streaked past him going down. Surprised, the dog tried to change direction in mid course. He stumbled. *Yes!* Salem thought. *Clumsy oaf!* He dashed into the living room, pausing just long enough to look around. *No safe places in here.*

He ran into the dining room, the kitten bouncing on his back. The dog was at his heels now. Salem could feel the beast's hot breath on his tail. *Faster,* Salem told himself, *or you're dog meat for sure.*

He dashed into the kitchen, looking around frantically. He leapt onto the counter, the Doberman snapping at his heels. *Yikes! This was way too close for comfort!* Without stopping to think, Salem sailed to the top of the refrigerator.

His heart was pounding so hard Salem thought it might explode. He turned to look back down at the dog. The Doberman growled and barked in frustration. *Still too close,* Salem thought. He made the short leap to the top of the cabinets.

There. The dog couldn't possibly reach them now.

"Nyah, nyah," Salem said breathlessly. He stuck out his tongue at the dog. "Can't get us now!" He shook his back a little, and the kitten slid off. She sat next to him, looking slightly dazed. "It's okay, fuzz-face," Salem assured her. "You're safe now."

"Hello?" The dog's owner walked into the kitchen. Salem snapped his mouth shut. He'd better not talk in front of this mortal.

"Hello?" the man said again, looking around. "That's funny. I would have sworn I heard someone talking in here."

The dog barked wildly.

The man looked up at the cabinets and chuckled. "What's the matter, Killer?" he asked. "Can't get at your little tidbit? That's okay, boy. I'll get her for ya."

Salem watched in horror as the man grabbed a chair and plopped it in front of the refrigerator. *He wouldn't!*

He would. The man climbed up on the chair and reached up for the kitten.

They were trapped!

Salem arched his back. He hissed. *Where is Sabrina when I need her?* he thought desperately.

"Cool it, there, kitty," the man said. "I ain't gonna hurt ya. I just want this little piece of fluff here, for Killer."

Salem hissed again. As the man reached past him, Salem swiped at the gloved hand, his claws unsheathed. *How could the man be so cruel?* Salem wondered. *What did the kitten ever do to him?*

Salem struck at the man again. It was no use, though. With those black gloves on, he hardly seemed to feel a thing. He

7 1

ignored Salem, calmly reaching past him and picking up the kitten.

There was nothing Salem could do. He watched in horror as the man stepped off the chair, the kitten in one hand.

As the man held the kitten out to the Doberman, Salem quickly turned his head and blocked his view with one paw. He couldn't look. It was just too awful. . . .

Chapter 10

Salem froze, waiting for the kitten's screams. *Make it quick,* he thought. *Then she won't suffer. Much.* He gulped.

But there was nothing. No pitiful meows for help. No screams.

Slowly, Salem turned his head and lowered his paw. He opened his eyes and peeked. He snapped his eyes shut. It was awful. The dog had the kitten in his mouth. He *was* going to eat her.

But what was that sound?
Purring?

Slowly, Salem opened his eyes and took a better look. Relief swept through him. The dog was sitting with the kitten between his feet. He was licking her head with his huge, slobbery tongue. And she *was* purring.

Ugh, Salem thought. *How can she purr with that beast slobbering all over her?* But there was no doubt about it. She loved it.

Salem felt relieved, and then indignant. *That's* my *kitten that dog is slobbering on! What gives him the right?* Salem completely forgot how much he'd wanted to get rid of her.

"You missed little Tidbit here, didn't ya, Killer?" the man said. He rubbed Killer's head, and the dog's tail thumped on the floor. "Well, don't you worry, boy. We'll take her home again. You'll have your pal back."

"Hey, what's this all about?" Sabrina walked into the kitchen. She dropped her backpack on the table. "Why is the front door wide open? Who are you?" she asked the man. "And what is that dog doing to my kitten?" She moved toward the kitten, arms outstretched to pick her up.

The dog let out a long, low growl.

Sabrina stopped.

"It's okay, boy," the man said. "Easy, now." He patted the dog's head. "Sorry," he said. "Killer thinks she's his kitten. She *is* his kitten, really. We lost her, about two weeks ago."

"Why didn't you come looking for her sooner, then?" Sabrina asked slowly. "We put flyers up."

"I know," the man said. He held up

the crumpled flyer. "But I didn't see this until today. We were looking for her near where we live, on the other side of town," the man explained. "I can't imagine how she got all the way over here." He shook his head.

"I don't know either," Sabrina said. "We found her out by our garbage can one night. It was pouring, so we brought her in."

"That was very nice of you," the man said. "I hate to think what might have happened to her if someone hadn't taken her in." He reached down and patted the dog on the head. "And I hate to think how bad Killer would feel if we hadn't found her. He's been miserable ever since she got lost."

Sabrina sighed. "We'd just about given up on anyone claiming her," she said. "I was beginning to think maybe I could keep her." She looked longingly at the kitten.

Salem jumped down to the top of the refrigerator. He meowed loudly, trying to get Sabrina's attention.

It worked. She walked over to him. He leaned forward and whispered in her ear. "Don't let him take the kitten if you want her," he said. "Put a spell on him. Make him forget."

Sabrina reached up and scratched his neck. "I can't do that," she whispered back. "It wouldn't be fair."

"Fair, schmair," Salem whispered back. "Don't you want to keep her?" He didn't want to admit it to Sabrina, but right now, *he* wanted to keep the kitten. *Why should that dog get to keep her? She adored* me!

Sabrina turned back around. "How can you be sure she's really your kitten?"

she asked. "Maybe she's just a kitten that looks like your Tidbit."

"Are you kidding?" the man asked. "How many kittens do you know will even go near a dog like Killer? Watch this." The man picked up the kitten and set her a few feet away from Killer. She ran right back to him and climbed up onto his back. Then she scrambled up on top of his head and lay down.

"That's her favorite spot," the man said.

Sabrina laughed. "I guess you're right," she said. She held her hands up in a gesture of defeat. "I'm sorry to see her go. But if she's yours, she's yours."

"Thanks," the man said. "Besides, it looks like you've already got a pretty nice cat of your own. He tried hard to protect Tidbit."

"Oh really?" Sabrina raised her eyebrows. "Imagine that." She turned and looked at Salem.

Uh-oh! Salem thought. *My cover's blown!*

"Well," the man said, "We'll be going now. Thanks for taking such good care of Tidbit. Killer and I appreciate it." He bent over and put on Killer's leash. Then he picked up the kitten and headed for the front door.

Salem jumped down to the floor. He followed Sabrina as she walked them out.

When Sabrina closed the front door behind them, she turned to Salem. "So you were protecting Tidbit, were you?" she said, smiling. "I knew it—you actually liked that kitten, didn't you?"

Salem put his nose in the air. "Of course not. The man was delusional. Obviously, anyone who dresses like that is a few doughnuts short of a dozen."

Sabrina giggled. "That was some get-up, all right." She plopped down on the couch. "I thought they were pretty scary-looking, to tell you the truth. If you stood up to the two of them, Salem, you are one brave cat."

Salem jumped up on the couch next to Sabrina. He puffed out his chest. "They didn't scare me one bit," he said.

"So you *did* try to protect the kitten," Sabrina said. "I *knew* it. You were jealous at first, but then she kind of grew on you. Admit it."

"Don't be ridiculous," Salem said. "I was only thinking of your feelings. I knew you liked the little hairball. I didn't want you to be upset, that's all."

"Uh-huh." Sabrina reached over and scratched Salem under the chin. "You old softie." She grinned at him, but then her smile faded. "It's going to seem strange not having the kitten around anymore. I *was* kind of attached to her."

"Ah, good riddance," Salem said gruffly. He didn't want to admit that he was going to miss her, too. Who would have thought that could happen? "She was more trouble than she was worth," he added, trying to convince himself.

"I wouldn't go that far," Sabrina said. "But maybe Aunt Zelda was right. Maybe witches should just have familiars, not pets."

"You think so?" Salem asked, pretending to be indifferent.

"Absolutely," Sabrina said. "She was cute, but cute isn't everything."

"True," Salem agreed.

"For example, she was completely useless when it came to witch stuff," Sabrina said. She pointed her finger, and a pizza box appeared on the coffee table in front of them. "Didn't know one spell from another."

"You're right about that," Salem said. The smell of pepperoni and anchovies rose from the box in front of him. His mouth watered.

"And her advice about boys—forget it," Sabrina went on. "She knew next to nothing about them."

"I have to admit, you've got a point," Salem said. His stomach growled loudly.

"Not only that, she wasn't much fun to share a pizza with," Sabrina said. She pointed at the table again, and two plates appeared.

"Yeah," Salem grumbled. "She ate all the good parts."

The pizza box opened, and a slice floated onto a plate. The plate sailed through the air to Salem.

"For the number-one cat in the Spellman household," Sabrina said. "And my favorite feline." She reached over and scratched his neck.

"You mean *me?*" Salem felt flushed with pleasure.

"Of course," Sabrina said. "That little fluff brain couldn't hold a candle to you, you know."

"Of course not," Salem said. He took a big bite of pizza smothered with anchovies. "I knew that all along."

Cat Care Tips

#1 If you are going to bring another cat into your house, be sure that the new cat sees a veterinarian before it meets your cats. The veterinarian should check to make sure the new cat is healthy and does not have any diseases that can be passed on to your cat.

#2 Most cats do not like other cats that they do not know at first. It usually takes about two weeks for cats to get used to new cats.

#3 Never leave cats who do not know each other alone together—they will probably get into a big fight.

#4 Remember, be patient when you introduce the new cat. Even if the cats don't get along right away, they still may become great friends in time.

—Laura E. Smiley, MS, DVM, Dipl. ACVIM
Gwynedd Veterinary Hospital